The Magic Christmas Pony

Story by Regina Françoise Cooley   Illustrated by Hans Henrik Hansen

Capstone Publishing, Inc.
P.O. Box 1586
Bellingham, WA 98227

ISBN   1880450-04-6

Library of Congress Number 91-76342

The illustrations in this book were produced with tempera and watercolor on watercolor paper.

Text type is Goudy.

Color transparencies by Mark Bergsma, Bellingham, Washington.

Book typesetting and layout by Kate Weisel, Bellingham, Washington.

Color separations by Vision Graphics Inc., Ludlow, Maine.

Capstone Publishing, Inc.
Bellingham, Washington

For my children
Michael and Elizabeth Dunn and for
my husband Leland, with love.
R.F.C.

For all my girls
Maya, Sofie, and Emma, and my wife
Liv, with lots of love.
H.H.H.

Once upon a time there was a handsome carousel. It stood at the edge of a small town. To be exact, it sat in an open field that was the old county fairground.

The fairground and the carousel are long since gone, but in olden days when spring changed into summer, it was the happiest place to be for the town's children and their parents. Of course, that was really very long ago.

"How many years ago was it, Grandfather?" asked a young boy's voice coming from the great iron bedstead. Grandfather turned thoughtful and a few wrinkles settled deeper in his forehead as he tried to remember back through the years when, as a young boy, he had ridden the carousel astride his favorite pony.

Frederick brushed a tumble of light brown curls from his forehead and propped himself up on two fat pillows. His eager blue eyes fixed on his grandfather as the old man poked up the fire, then settled comfortably back in his easy chair.

Earlier in the day the whole family had helped trim the Christmas tree with tinsel and old-fashioned glass ornaments that had decorated the trees since grandfather's childhood.

Mother had brought in an old red lacquered chest from China. Inside, carefully wrapped in soft green silk, were nestled five gaily decorated cloisonné bells with hang rings. They too had travelled all the way from China many years ago. The children loved the old chest, and the bells were their favorite ornaments. Father, mother and grandfather had hung their bells high up on the tree.

Then it was the children's turn. Frederick and his sister, Valentina, had approached the chest and each had carefully lifted a bell. After they had fastened them to the tree, Valentina, her long honey-colored hair pulled back in a pony tail, stood on tip toe and gently shook the branches until the bells' clappers made a wonderful tinkling sound.

That evening, bedtime had come much too soon for Frederick and Valentina. Frederick was startled out of his daydream by grandfather clearing his throat, ready to continue the story. Henry the cat was dozing on his lap.

"I was about your age, Frederick, when I rode that carousel. Of all the rides, my favorite was the pony ride. The pony I liked best looked alive to me. He had a long white mane and a long, silky white tail. His tail was so long it almost reached to the ground.

"His body was covered with a colorful saddle blanket. The pony's large, brown eyes were warm and friendly. His head was tilted toward me, and his mouth was half open as though he wanted to say, 'Get those feet in the stirrups, young man, and hold on for here we go!'

"When the calliope music started, the carousel would go around and around, faster and faster. My pony would prance, with his mane and tail flying in the breeze, and his eyes would flash joyfully. At that very moment I was certain he really could fly. I felt I could ride anywhere in the world with him.

"Then, one day, when I went to the carousel for another ride, the pony was gone! I looked around frantically until I found the carousel operator. Not even he could imagine what had happened. My beautiful friend had vanished without a trace.

"I was heartbroken. Months went by. Then I heard there was a rumor abroad that the missing pony had been seen here and there by children who had also loved him. Most parents smiled and set it down to childish imagination."

Grandfather interrupted his story when he heard deep breathing coming from the bed. He rose quietly because Frederick had slipped into a deep slumber. Smiling, he tip-toed from the room.

Outside, one could still hear the clear high voices of the carolers going from door to door, but inside the house all was quiet. The flaring embers in the fireplace cast strange shadows on the faces of a squadron of wooden soldiers standing guard on top of the toy chest. The building blocks stacked in the opposite corner of the room seemed to take on gigantic proportions. Downstairs, the hallway clock started chiming, one-two-three—twelve times in all. At the same time the bells in the church steeples were tolling.

Suddenly, Frederick sat bolt upright, not knowing what had awakened him. He cocked his ear and held his breath. A strange sound seemed to be coming from downstairs. The noise grew louder and louder. For certain, someone—or something—was coming up the stairs.

Frederick bit his lower lip. He always bit his lower lip when he was frightened. Now, he was very frightened indeed!

The clattering noise coming up the stairway was unlike anything he had ever heard in the house. Abruptly, it stopped—right in front of his bedroom door!

For a brief moment there was total silence. Then, the door flew open and there stood the carousel pony! Frederick blinked in disbelief. The pony stepped inside and came to the bed.

"Don't be afraid, Frederick," he said in a reassuring voice. "Please get your sister at once."

In a flash, Frederick was down the hall and back, holding the hand of a very sleepy Valentina. She rubbed her big brown eyes and stared in awe at the pony. Frederick slipped a protective arm around his sister's shoulder.

The pony spoke again in a soothing voice.

"I am The Magic Christmas Pony," he said, "I can fly you northeast to Russia, east to Prussia, north to Scandinavia, or south to Old Belgravia. But tonight, my young friends, we are going west, back in time, to Old China and its capital city, Peking. There we will meet my close friend, the Dragon of Fantasy. He can make the most wonderful things happen."

Valentina and Frederick cried out as one. "Please, we don't want to see any dragons. They frighten us!"

The Pony replied, "Don't be frightened. You will love the Chinese dragons. They are the friendliest dragons in the whole world. Trust me, my young friends, you will see."

Frederick asked The Magic Pony, "How are we going to get to China!"

The Magic Pony chuckled and replied, "Leave that up to me, my boy." First I want you children to stand up on the bed.

"Frederick, you climb onto my back." He turned to Valentina and said, "Hop on, young lady, put your arms around your brother and hold on tightly."

The Magic Pony faced the large double window, concentrated all of his thoughts, and then it happened. The window flew open and the pony made one big leap. The next moment the three of them were sailing up into the sky. Thousands of stars lit up the countryside below.

The children looked down and saw roof tops galore and a world covered with snow. They sped over fields, fences and stables, over tree tops and hedges and homes with gables.

Faster and faster they flew, climbing higher and higher, so high Frederick and Valentina felt they could touch the moon.

The only other travelers in that great sky were flocks of migrating geese flapping their strong wings as they cast ghostly shadows across the face of the moon. And there was the wind, tugging at Frederick's pajamas, billowing Valentina's ruffled nightgown and playfully tossing about The Magic Pony's mane and tail.

Until this moment, they had travelled in silence. The children were awe-struck and the pony was preoccupied with remembering the directions to China. A long time had passed since he last had visited his dragon friend.

Now the pony spoke. "Frederick and Valentina, we are rapidly approaching China and the Great Wall. It will guide us to Peking and the Forbidden City."

They flew over many rugged mountains and serpentine rivers. Then they saw it, the Great Wall of China! It looked like a gigantic dragon winding its way as far as the eye could see. Valentina asked The Magic Pony, "How long is the wall?"

He replied, "My dear Valentina, the wall is about one thousand six hundred miles long, as the crow flies, and it is almost thirty feet high." The Magic Pony descended rapidly. Below them were lovely pagodas of different sizes and shapes with moats and graceful stone bridges. Soon the pony pointed out the magnificent Imperial Palace with its brilliant yellow roof.

Suddenly, waiting for them on top of the Great Entrance Gate, they saw the Dragon of Fantasy. The children were speechless. It was the first time they had ever seen a real dragon. How splendid he was!

Before they realized it, the pony landed and the dragon came forward to greet them.

Every time he moved his head, it sounded like a hundred small bells were ringing. When he twisted his body and switched his tail it looked like he was wearing all of the colors of the rainbow at once.

The Magic Pony and the Dragon of Fantasy embraced each other. Then Valentina and Frederick were properly introduced. The Dragon told the children they had arrived just in time to go to the great Banquet Hall where they would meet some of China's most famous dragons. There was a friendly twinkle in his eyes when he added, "The Forbidden City is a place filled with surprises. It is a maze of palaces, temples, courtyards and gardens. You must stay close to your attendants otherwise you will be lost."

The Dragon made a clicking sound. Almost at once four court attendants arrived with two strange-looking chairs. Each chair was carried on poles by two attendants, one in front and one behind. The children did not know it then, but later the pony told them they were called sedan chairs.

Valentina and Frederick learned quickly that they had to sit perfectly still and absolutely straight, or the chair would tilt this way and that way. The result could be a very strange feeling in their stomachs.

The children saw the most fascinating sights in the huge courtyard. They passed several high court officials dressed in long green silk robes decorated with white cranes and golden pheasants.

Frederick was fascinated by the court chamberlains on horseback. Their loose, beautifully embroidered ceremonial gowns covered both the saddle and the stirrups.

They passed enormous bronze censers, some in the form of a huge bird called a Phoenix. Others looked like gigantic tortoises, and from all of them rose billows of fragrant smoke.

The children also saw many flower beds and ancient pine trees from whose limbs hung ornate cages containing colorful birds. Finally, they came to a long row of low buildings used as waiting rooms. The court attendants conducted Frederick and Valentina to one of them and told them to wait.

They hardly had time to look around when two servant girls came in. Each was carrying a bowl of water, towels and a dish containing delicately sculptured miniature soaps. The water and the soap dish were placed in front of them.

The children gratefully washed their faces and hands and dried them on the soft towels.

Two male court attendants entered with beautiful silk garments, one for Frederick and one for Valentina. They also handed each of them a pair of silk slipper-like shoes. The children were delighted with their new clothing.

Valentina's gown was green, embroidered all over with pink and red hollyhocks and trimmed with gold braid. Her shoes were the same shade of green as her gown. Decorating the toes were two impish little golden dragons.

Frederick's garment was a loose, red ceremonial robe with purple borders on the sleeves and hem. On the back of his robe embroidered in gold thread was a large four-clawed dragon. Frederick's shoes were made of purple silk worked with a border of golden dragon claws.

The court attendants said to the children, "There is one very important custom you must learn. It is called 'Kowtowing.' We will show you how to do it."

Frederick and Valentina looked very clumsy trying it the first time. It was such a funny sight watching the children as they tried to kneel and touch their foreheads to the ground that it made the attendants giggle. Later, Valentina told the pony that it was very tiring. "Touching our heads to the ground made us dizzy until we got used to it," she explained.

One of the attendants said, "Children, you must kowtow when you meet the Imperial Dragon. He is the only dragon in China who has five claws and whose likeness is embroidered on Their Majesties' robes."

The attendants led the children to the great banquet hall where they were reunited with The Magic Pony and the Dragon of Fantasy. The Pony was delighted. "Valentina and Frederick," he exclaimed, "how attractive you are in your new clothes!" The sound of a great gong filled the hall. Instantly an enormous screen was folded back and there at the head of the longest table they had ever seen sat the Imperial Dragon.

He was the most magnificent dragon in the banquet hall. He seemed as bright as the sun, a shimmery gold from head to tail. His eyes flashed like two great diamonds. The Dragon of Fantasy introduced the children.

Frederick and Valentina kowtowed gracefully. The Imperial Dragon said, "I welcome you, Frederick and Valentina, to the special ceremonial banquet of the dragons. Thanks to the pony and my noble friend, the Dragon of Fantasy, this is the first occasion on which non-dragons have been invited to our gathering. It gives me great pleasure to present you to the assembly of Chinese dragons. Let the banquet begin!"

A smaller dragon known as the Dragon of the Bells struck some cymbals and pleasant, ringing sounds echoed throughout the hall.

Valentina and Frederick were seated next to the River Dragon. His body was a magnificent jade green. His eyes sparkled like rubies. He was a very chatty sort of dragon. He told the children, "My picture is carved on the parapets of all the bridges that cross the rivers in China. You can see I am a dragon of consequence—one of great responsibility." The children nodded in agreement.

On the other side, their dinner companion was the Incense Dragon. He told the children, "I love smoke. That is why you can find me adorning so many incense burners." While he spoke a fragrant smoke cloud curled from his nose and wafted over the table.

Across from Frederick and Valentina sat a dragon who was almost invisible. He whispered to them, "I am the Bashful Dragon. It is very difficult for anyone to see me, for I appear mostly on closed doors."

Next to the Bashful Dragon sat a ferocious appearing dragon. When he spoke to the children his long, fiery tongue almost leaped across the table. He said, "I am the strongest of all China's dragons and, because my face looks like a fearsome tiger, people are afraid of me. That is why I guard the entrances to jails."

His yellow eyes twinkled when he added, "But appearances can be deceiving. By nature, I am really very sweet." The children were relieved.

At the head of the table, next to the Imperial Dragon, sat the Dragon of Fantasy. Next to him sat his friend The Magic Pony. Beside the pony sat a most glorious specimen of dragonhood. His body was covered in pearly, iridescent scales..His eyes seemed to be made of mother of pearl.

He told the pony, "I am the Sea Dragon. I traverse the South China Sea, the East China Sea and the Yellow Sea. I watch over the waves, the tides, the storms, the sea creatures and the ocean treasures. You can see what a busy dragon I am."

The pony could not agree with him more. He told the Sea Dragon how very much he admired him.

The banquet table was covered with a saffron brocade cloth. Three enormous porcelain bowls were heaped with mandarin oranges. The dragons considered them a great delicacy.

Some of the dishes and bowls were ornamented with green dragons, others with beautiful flowers. Valentina was fascinated by the golden dragon menu holders, and the peach shaped silver saucers filled with almonds and dried watermelon seeds.

Frederick and Valentina watched the dragons use silver chopsticks and very soon learned how to manage theirs. Both of the young visitors were delighted with the abundance of cakes baked in all sorts of imaginative shapes.

Delicate blue and white porcelain jars, filled to their rims with candied ginger, stood next to each place. Other jars were filled with candied cherries, persimmons, loquats and freshly peeled litchi nuts.

After eating their fill of Chinese delicacies, everyone was pleased. The children smiled and thanked the Imperial Dragon.

The Dragon of the Bells stood up. He was about to strike the cymbals, when a great commotion was heard outside the banquet hall. Suddenly, the large doors burst open and the captain of the Imperial Guard appeared dressed in his gleaming golden armor. Buckled around his middle was a large jewel-encrusted sword.

A strange silence fell over the dragons. For a moment, the captain stood perfectly still. Then, his eyes fixed on Frederick and Valentina. He raised his sword and signaled. Immediately, two of his men marched in and took their places beside him. Then he lowered his sword and snapped in a commanding voice, "Take the children away!"

The Magic Christmas Pony, the Dragon of Fantasy and the Imperial Dragon exchanged glances. Then, before they could say a word, each guard took a frightened child by the arm and followed the captain out of the hall.

Valentina's voice trembled as she whispered, "I'm really scared, Frederick. Do you think we're being arrested?"

Frederick, in an effort to sound brave, replied, "But we haven't done anything wrong."

"Maybe," Valentina said, "The Magic Christmas Pony should not have brought us here." Her brother saw her shiver as she added, "I hope he comes quickly to explain."

The guards led the children swiftly along pebble covered paths. Fearing the worst, they hardly noticed the beauty around them, the Empress's Peony Mountain—a large mound covered with red, pink and white blossoms. Over it fluttered a cloud of yellow butterflies with spotted wings. In the distance they could hear the shrill cries of the Imperial Peacocks.

Urged by the guards, the children moved onto a narrow, stone bridge that arched over a running brook whose banks were planted with weeping willow trees. Periwinkle colored dragon flies darted here and there over the water.

From behind a low wall on their right came the sound of a horse whinnying. The children were hopeful. Maybe it was The Magic Christmas Pony coming to the rescue! Valentina caught a glimpse of several beautiful Mongolian ponies. Some were white and some were gray and they all had long flowing manes and tails. But why, Valentina thought, couldn't it have been   their pony?

Frederick and Valentina were led from the Weeping Willow Woods to a magnificent building. The guards escorted them through an entrance way and they found themselves in a great hall.

At the far end stood a huge screen, carved from top to bottom with intertwined golden dragons. In front of it, seated on their elevated thrones, were their majesties, the Emperor and Empress of China.

Valentina was entranced. She had never seen anyone so beautifully dressed. The Empress wore a sky blue silk gown covered with embroidered red peonies. Her headdress was made of pearl and jade flowers. On her fingers were many rings and long gold fingernail protectors. Her tiny silk shoes were trimmed with small pearl tassels. The Emperor was wearing his Imperial Dragon robe and headdress.

On either side of the thrones stood a tall, slender post. On top of each a golden tulip-shaped holder was fastened. From each of them rose a giant fan fashioned of peacock feathers.

The children were speechless when they realized where they were. They glanced at the expressionless face of the captain of the guard but could see nothing to reassure them. Frederick wondered, would they ever be allowed to leave?

The Empress spoke briefly to the captain who urged the children forward. When they hesitated she motioned them to approach the throne.

Frederick took Valentina by the hand and drew her closer to him. "Remember," he whispered, "we must kowtow and do it properly. I don't know what they are going to do to us but if we're nice and polite, it may help."

The children stopped a few feet from the throne and kowtowed exactly as they were taught. To their vast relief, the Empress smiled and reached for their hands. In perfect English she said, "Welcome to the Garden Palace, children. It pleases us that you have learned to kowtow so well."

Then she introduced them to the Emperor and again, they were welcomed graciously. "Where is your beautiful pony?" he asked.

Frederick replied, "Your Majesty, he must still be with our dragon friends." Whereupon the Emperor and Empress exchanged pleased glances. The Emperor nodded to the Captain of the guard who left the throne room and returned almost immediately with the pony and led him to the children. Frederick and Valentina were so relieved to see him that they hugged his neck. The pony placed one foot forward and bowed his head. Their Majesties clasped their hands together with delight. The Empress turned to the children and said, "How charming! Even our Imperial ponies are not so well mannered."

The Emperor clapped his hands lightly and two court attendants materialized from behind the screen. Each carried a richly embroidered cushion, which they placed at the foot of the Empress' throne.

"We have asked you here to share a special Palace entertainment," said the Emperor. "Have your pony stand over here beside me and you two please be seated."

When the visitors were settled, a great gong sounded. Speaking in a commanding voice, the Emperor said, "Let the performances begin!"

Without warning, the Great Throne Room was filled with the deafening crash of cymbals. A troupe of colorfully dressed acrobats came tumbling onto the large stage. They performed feats that seemed humanly impossible.

Meanwhile, on a smaller stage, jugglers tossed brightly-painted plates, real fruit, small flags and flaming torches until the air was filled with flying objects. Incredibly, not a single one was dropped.

Chinese flower fairies dressed in white and red, wearing headdresses made of real flowers, danced to the music of a dozen flutes.

It was all so exciting that Frederick and Valentina hoped it would never end. Happily, there was more to come. Mongolian Dancers leaped into view, whirling to the sound of their ancient instruments.

The Empress leaned forward and in a soft voice said, "Watch carefully now, children. The Imperial Dancers are going to perform one of China's oldest court dances. You will see why we call it the Water Sleeve."

Frederick and Valentina were fascinated as a shimmering silk curtain parted revealing row upon row of dancers who glided onto the stage in the strangest costumes they had ever seen. The costumes completely covered the dancers' heads and necks, then flowed in a most unusual way to conceal their arms and hands in long, narrow, ribbon-like sleeves. The bodices of the dresses were draped in a crisscross fashion in such a way that the skirts hung in graceful folds.

Moving in time to the music, the dancers' arms rose and fell. Their long silk sleeves floated to simulate the motion of ocean waves.

Suddenly there was an earsplitting explosion of firecrackers that nearly made the children jump off their cushions. Their surprise amused Their Majesties, for nothing delights the Chinese more than the sound of exploding firecrackers. The explosions signaled the entrance of the Dancing Dragons.

Frederick and Valentina laughed with the others when the dragons moved across the stage with their great eyes rolling in a most comical way as they sought to keep their tails from tangling.

They pretended to confront each other ferociously as they jumped about. Finally, they all joined claws and faced the Emperor and Empress and their guests. The audience shrieked with delight as great clouds of colored smoke erupted from their nostrils.

Over the popping of the firecrackers, Frederick shouted, "I like these dancing dragons best of all!" It was also the Emperor's favorite dance. The Dragon Dance ended the entertainment.

When the last of the firecrackers had exploded, the Empress asked the children if they had enjoyed the festivities.

"Your Majesty," Valentina replied, "I have never seen anything so beautiful." Frederick agreed. "I will tell all my friends about it," he added.

The Emperor and Empress smiled, then took their hands and wished Frederick and Valentina a safe journey back to their homeland.

In the courtyard again, The Magic Christmas Pony said, "Let us make haste so you can be back with your family in time to open your Christmas gifts."

The Dragon of Fantasy was waiting for them at the gate. He presented the children with two gifts wrapped in bright red paper. "These gifts, dear children, are in memory of your visit to the Forbidden City. You were both perfect guests. I will miss you."

Valentina stood on tip-toe and kissed the Dragon's nose.

"Thank you," she said, "I will never forget you."

Frederick bowed and said, "Thank you for your hospitality. Please come and visit us. We will take good care of you."

The Pony embraced his friend and in no time at all, they were on their way.

When Frederick and Valentina looked back, the Dragon of Fantasy had returned to his place on the roof. As they waved good-bye, both children were certain they saw two big tears running down his cheeks.

Back home the bells were ringing in the church steeples. Mouth-watering breakfast smells wafted all through the house. Grandfather stood by the Christmas tree and mused aloud, "This is the first Christmas morning I remember the children sleeping so late."

Mother overheard him and said, "I'll go and wake the sleepy heads." As she spoke, down the staircase came Frederick. He smiled when he saw his grandfather. Close behind him came Valentina, her brown eyes still looked sleepy. In the crook of her arm sat Henry, the cat, looking very festive with a bright green ribbon tied in a bow around his neck.

The family all wished each other a Merry Christmas. The house rang with expressions of delight as the packages were opened.

Grandfather pointed to two bright red packages that were nearly concealed behind a drooping lower branch of the Christmas tree.

"Where did those come from?" he asked. Father and mother shook their heads. "We have no idea."

While the curious grownups watched, Valentina and Frederick removed the paper from the mysterious gifts.

In each package they discovered identical lacquered boxes. The children opened them. Inside they found two beautifully carved, apple-green jade dragon figures.

They gasped and exclaimed, "It's our friend, the Dragon of Fantasy!"

Grandfather was as mystified as the children's parents.

"But children, how do you know this is the Dragon of Fantasy?" he asked.

"We met him last night," Frederick replied, "Didn't we, Valentina?"

Before she could answer, Grandfather gave them a knowing smile. "But of course you did. You met the Dragon of Fantasy in your dreams!"

The children exchanged amused glances and decided not to say anything more. Neither Frederick nor Valentina ever wanted to hurt dear Grandfather, for everyone, especially grownups, should remember that if you dream hard enough, dreams really do come true.

Suddenly, through the big windows, the children saw The Magic Christmas Pony again. He nodded and smiled and then, magically, he was gone…

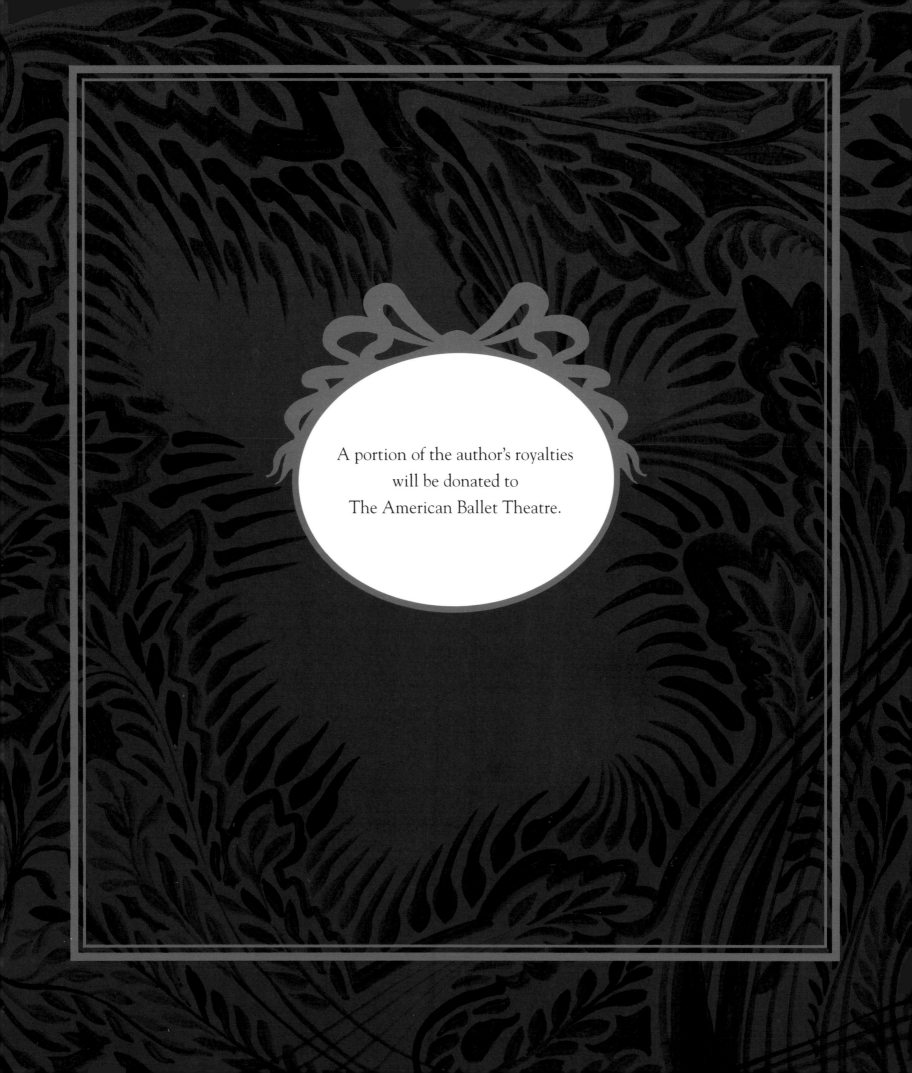